2004

E
GRA
o circs

Gray, Libba Moore.

My mama had a dancing
heart.

13
7/2010

$15.99

DATE			

My Mama Had a Dancing Heart

by Libba Moore Gray

illustrated by Raúl Colón

Orchard Books
New York

*For my four children, who through the years
have made my heart dance*

*For Ann Tobias . . . and for the
Appalachian Ballet Company*   *L.M.G.*

For José and Maria   *R.C.*

Text copyright © 1995 by Libba Moore Gray

Illustrations copyright © 1995 by Raúl Colón

Orchard Books
95 Madison Avenue
New York, NY 10016

Manufactured in the United States of America
Printed by Barton Press, Inc. Bound by Horowitz/Rae. Book design by Chris Hammill Paul.

10   9   8   7   6   5   4   3   2   1

The text of this book is set in 17 point Perpetua.
The illustrations are done on watercolor paper and combine watercolor washes, etching,
and the use of colored pencils and litho pencils.

Library of Congress Cataloging-in-Publication Data

Gray, Libba Moore.
My mama had a dancing heart / by Libba Moore Gray ; illustrated by Raúl Colón.
p. cm.
"A Melanie Kroupa book"—Half t.p.
Summary: A ballet dancer recalls how she and her mother would welcome each season with a dance outdoors.
ISBN 0-531-09470-7. —ISBN 0-531-08770-0 (lib. bdg.)
[1. Dancing—Fiction. 2. Mothers and daughters—Fiction. 3. Seasons—Fiction.] I. Colón, Raúl, ill. II. Title.
PZ7.G7793My 1995
[Fic]—dc20
94-48802

My mama had a dancing heart
and she shared that heart with me.

With a grin and a giggle,
a hug and a whistle,
we'd slap our knees
and Mama would say:
"Bless the world
it feels like
a tip-tapping
song-singing
finger-snapping
kind of day.
Let's celebrate!"
And so we did.

When a warm spring rain
would come pinging on the windowpane,
we'd kick off our shoes
and out into the rain we'd go.

We'd dance
a frog-hopping
leaf-growing
flower-opening
hello spring ballet.

High-stepping and splashing,
the rain running down our faces,
I'd slip-swish behind Mama
through the newly green grass.

And afterward
we'd read rain poems
and drink sassafras tea
with lemon curls floating.

And in summer
when the waves would come
plash-splashing on the shore,
out we'd go into the red-orange morning
with kites and balloons
tied to our wrists.

We'd do a seabird-flapping
dolphin-arching
hello summer ballet,
with me following Mama,
the sand stuck between the toes
of our up-and-down squish-squashing feet.

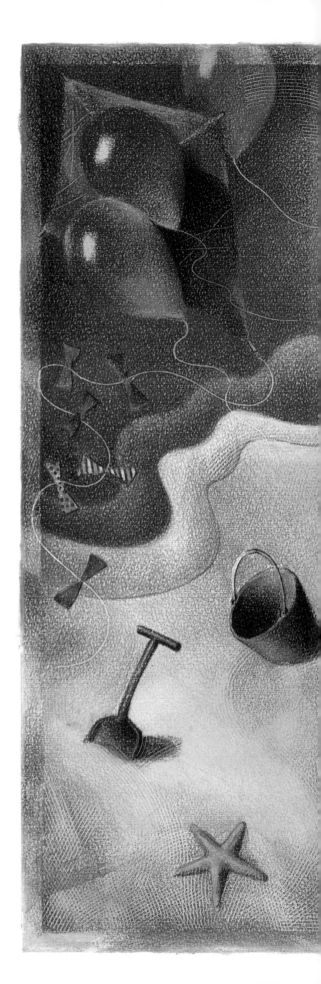

And afterward
we'd seashell-pile the windowsill
and drink lemonade cold.

*A*nd when the cool autumn winds
would come puff-puffing
through the clouds,
and the hold-on-tight leaves
would finally let go and float-flutter
to the ground,

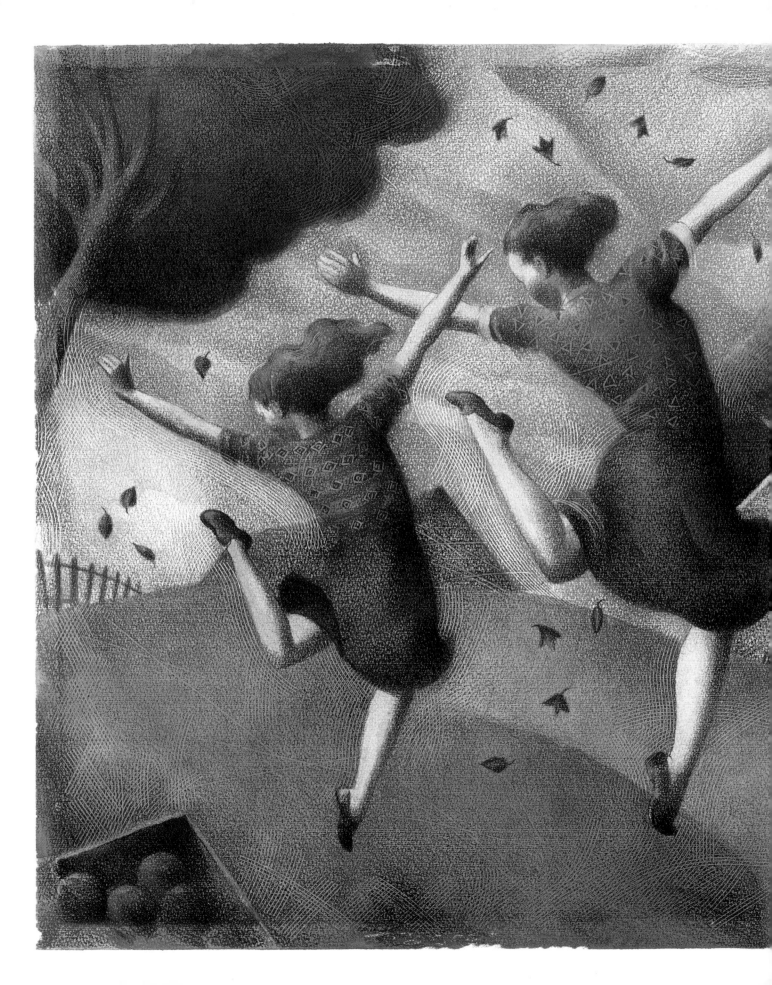

out we'd go into the eye-blinking blue air,
with Mama leading in a leaf-kicking
leg-lifting
hand-clapping
hello autumn ballet.

And afterward
we'd wax paper—press leaves
red and gold
and drink hot tea spiced.

*A*nd when the winter snows
came softly down
shawling the earth,

out we'd go
and do a body-flat
arms-moving-up-and-down
snow-angel
hello winter ballet.

And then we'd stand up,
Mama first,
and dance in slow motion,
like hand-mittened
galoshes-galumphing
funny old snowmen.

And afterward
we'd cut snowflakes
paper-white delicate
and sip cocoa
with marshmallows floating.

$\mathcal{A}$nd now

after satin-ribboning my feet

and listening to the violins

sing-swelling

around me,

onto the stage I go

air-daring

leap-flying

wing-soaring

letting the
spring rain
summer waves
autumn leaves
winter snow
carry me along until
the music slows
and I feather-float
down . . . down
to the ground.

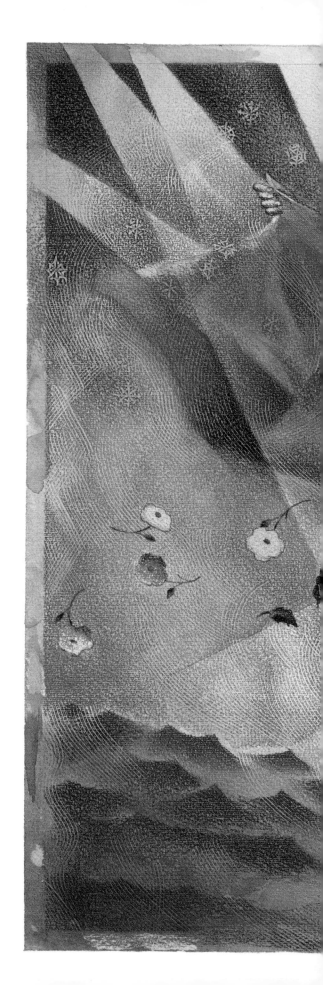

And afterward
I imagine that
I hear my mama saying:
"Bless the world
it feels like
a tip-tapping
song-singing
finger-snapping
kind of day.
Let's celebrate!"

My mama had a dancing heart
and she shared that heart with me.